The Chicken

And

The Egg

Hit the Road

By
Beatrice Ann

EDEN HOUSE/ NEW YORK

To Willie Beatrice Webber— *a woman of quiet courage— who shared her wealth of wit and wisdom with the world.*

You will never be forgotten.

In loving memory of JB

The Chicken and the Egg were riding in a car.
Were they going near? Were they going far?
They could not know how long it would be,
Just a winding road, as far as the eye could see.

What are we doing?

Where are we going?

When will we get there?

How will it be?

Who will we see?

Why must I wait? It's not fair!

"Please calm down," said Chicken to Egg.
"What are you worrying about?
You can scream and shout.
You can pull your hair out,
Or just relax instead."

"Oh, how much longer?" begged the Egg.
"I'm trying to be good,
But I'm sitting here and I don't like it.
I've done all I could."

"Oh, really?" Chicken asked.
"Are you doing all you can?
All I hear is whimpering and whining and wailing.
Was *that* your plan?"

"Well, I'm bored!" cried the Egg.
"What am I supposed to do?
I want to skip and run and play,
Not sit around with you."

"Yes, I know,"
Chicken replied.
"You want this ride
To be done.
And somehow you think
That moaning and groaning
Will make it SO much more fun?"

"No, I don't!" the Egg did say.
"I'm terribly tired. That's all."

"Well, I can't tell!"
The Chicken did yell,
"When all I hear is you bawl.
Why don't you choose
To do something new.
You've been doing this for a while.
Keep it up
And you might get stuck,
Never finding a reason to smile."

"Don't you look up ahead?" said the Egg.
"There are bumps in this road.
How can you be so quiet and calm,
When I'm hopping around like a toad?

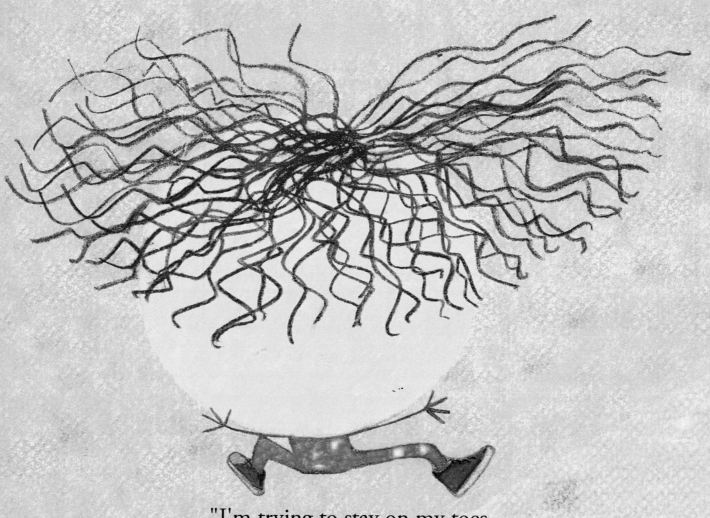

"I'm trying to stay on my toes,
While being knocked to and fro.

"One moment, I'm flying high!
Next, I'm falling down low..."

"Yes," said Chicken. "It's not so easy. This is something I know.
I've hit so many bumps and stumps; you could call me a pro!"

"Sometimes though,"
The Chicken did crow.
"You'll have to take it slow,
Or sit right down,
Look around,
'Til it's time again to go."

So, Little Egg sat and looked around.
And as the egg sat, more questions were found,
Questions and fears of how winds may shift,
That pesky little question: "What if? **WHAT IF?!**"

"**WHAT IF**," cried Egg, "we're stuck here all day?
What if a bear comes and chases us away?
What if a big cat bites us right where we sit?"
"What if," replied Chicken, "you're just throwing a fit?"

"What if we find **berries** to share with that bear?

What if we find **cubs** in that big cat's lair?

What if a little bunny leads us to a **waterfall?**

"What if we doze off, in the *SUNLIGHT*, and that's all?"

"Why don't you look at the butterflies and the bumblebees?
Smell the fresh air. Feel the cool breeze.
Watch as the birds soar swiftly by the trees.
How lucky we are! Wouldn't you agree?"

"I can agree," said Egg, "if you can agree with me.
The things that frighten most are the things I *cannot* see.
It's not so simple to simply let it be,
When the road that leads to roses can also lead to stormy sea."

"Perhaps," said Chicken. "Perhaps we can *never* know.
Sometimes The Unknown is the place we have to go.
How else can we grow? How else can we learn more,
If we never choose to go to where we've never been before?"

"Will this ride end though?" Egg wanted to know.

"Sure as the tide does flow," Chicken told Egg so.
"It's best if you just enjoy it. Enjoy it while you can.
You may never, ever be on such a ride like this again."

"When I was a little egg," Chicken said, "like you, I couldn't see.
But now I know, just because something IS doesn't mean it will *always* be.
Everything changes. Can't you see, even you and me?

"Even
The deepest
Tunnel
Comes to an end,
Eventually."

"Still, it's much too long of a road," cried Egg.
" I fear what lies ahead.
I don't want to go on.
I want to be done
And shut my eyes, instead.
All I see is darkness: DARKNESS all around."

"True," Chicken said,
"But LIGHT follows the dark; I've found.
It may seem far away.
It might seem out of reach.
But, I tell you: if you just keep searching,
You'll find what you seek."

"What do you know!"
Said the Egg.
"It was right underneath my nose.
The light never went out.
I just had my eyes closed.

"I can see clearly now.
What would crying do?
If I let my eyes
Fill with tears,
I might miss this view."

"What a smart little egg,"
Chicken said,
"But remember this my friend:
Every time a journey ends,
Another one begins."

"Hooray! We're here!"
Little Egg cheered.
"At last, we have arrived!

"But, what happens next?
Can anyone guess?"

"Why don't you decide?"

So...
It BEGINS

To Worry,

Egg worries a lot.
What worries you?

Or Not to Worry,
Chicken doesn't worry.
What helps you not to worry?

THAT is the question.

Worry

Draw a circle
around the one
that *you* should do.
YOU DECIDE!

Worry NOT